Tale of the Concrete City

Abdolhai Shammasi

TSL Publications

First published in Great Britain in 2024
By TSL Publications, Rickmansworth

ISBN: 978-1-915660-97-8

Cover design
Abbas Barghashi

Characters:

ARCHITECT

SURVEYOR

BLIND MAN

YOUNG MAN

YOUNG WOMAN

GNOME = THAT PERSON

It's night. A dry, unproductive, endless salt desert landscape is seen in the cold, misty moonlight. On one side of the stage, there is a civil engineering office with some drawing and surveying instruments, including a surveying tripod, a drawing table and many rolled up plans. On the other side of the stage, there are two beds, two chests of drawers, and two sofas. The sound of a bulldozer is hear. The ARCHITECT *is busy drawing and the* SURVEYOR *is repairing his theodolite.*

ARCHITECT:	Hell... Bloody hell... You're getting on my nerves.
SURVEYOR:	What a nuisance! This damned thing is out of order... Hey! Come and hold the screw for me, I want to fix the spring.
ARCHITECT:	Shut up, you bastard!
SURVEYOR:	[*Protesting.*] Did I say something wrong?
ARCHITECT:	You?! No!
SURVEYOR:	But I did. And you told me to shut up!
ARCHITECT:	[*Doing his work.*] I heard nothing.
SURVEYOR:	So, why did you tell me to shut up?
ARCHITECT:	[*Doing his work calmly.*] I didn't mean you.
SURVEYOR:	[*Looks around.*] There isn't anybody here but us, is there?
ARCHITECT:	Yes, there is... This bloody noise which seems to be endless. It makes me mad.
SURVEYOR:	Just don't care about it. Bit by bit you will get used to it.
ARCHITECT:	I am beginning to be frightened of it.
SURVEYOR:	I told you to pay no attention to it.
ARCHITECT:	It is impossible, isn't it?
SURVEYOR:	You can do nothing else.

ARCHITECT:	Tonight, the noise is heard from somewhere closer.
SURVEYOR:	Is it? I didn't notice it.
ARCHITECT:	How come you didn't notice it?
SURVEYOR:	I was busy doing my work. Mind your own business. You'll find it helps. Do you understand? Now come here and help me fix the spring.
ARCHITECT:	[*Approaches the* SURVEYOR.] But I can't ignore it.
SURVEYOR:	Seems it doesn't exist at all if you don't hear it.
ARCHITECT:	Just like that?
SURVEYOR:	Exactly... Now come and hold the spring. [*Goes behind his desk and is restless working. Crumples a piece of paper and tosses it into the garbage can. Puts the theodolite on the ground helplessly.*] I can't... I can't repair it.
ARCHITECT:	Because of the noise?
SURVEYOR:	[*Picks up the theodolite again.*] What?
ARCHITECT:	Nothing... [*Gets up and moves to the middle of the stage. Pauses for a while, stifled.*] I have butterflies in my stomach.
SURVEYOR:	Take it easy... Busy yourself with your work.
ARCHITECT:	I can't... I don't feel like working. I have a bad feeling.
SURVEYOR:	What?! A bad feeling?
ARCHITECT:	I have... I have a bad feeling... What's going to happen at last? What do you think?
SURVEYOR:	I must repair it. We have too much work to do tomorrow.

ARCHITECT:	I feel we're in danger.
SURVEYOR:	Danger?!
ARCHITECT:	Yeah… [*Looks around carefully and approaches the* SURVEYOR.] We should take care of ourselves.
SURVEYOR:	I think you are daydreaming … Ah … it's slipped.
ARCHITECT:	Slipped?! What?
SURVEYOR:	[*Puts down the theodolite and begins to crawl about on all fours.*] I was distracted… It slipped out of my hand. Now, how can I find such a little spring?
ARCHITECT:	You should have been more careful.
SURVEYOR:	I was. But the screw was not fixed properly. [*Touches the ground and moves on all fours in the middle of the stage.*] What if I can't find it?
ARCHITECT:	Where do you think it is?
SURVEYOR:	I don't know…
ARCHITECT:	I think it's quite close by.
SURVEYOR:	I know, that's why I am looking for it here.
ARCHITECT:	For what?
SURVEYOR:	It's obvious, for the spring.
ARCHITECT:	But I wasn't talking about the spring.
SURVEYOR:	So, what do you think I am looking for?
ARCHITECT:	The bulldozer… It must be quite close by.
SURVEYOR:	[*Puts his ear on the floor.*] That's right. As if it is just underneath us.
ARCHITECT:	[*Sits at his drawing table.*] That's why it sounds so loud.

SURVEYOR:	[*Looks for the spring on all fours again.*] It should be somewhere here.
ARCHITECT:	I think so. Have you ever seen it?
SURVEYOR:	Do you think I am blind? It was in my hand right now.
ARCHITECT:	Why do you mock me?
SURVEYOR:	I was answering your question.
ARCHITECT:	[*Concentrates on a drawing.*] If I could make it...
SURVEYOR:	Impossible! It will come up when it wishes. Don't worry.
ARCHITECT:	But it has to...
SURVEYOR:	It won't leave there unless all the foundations of the city collapse.
ARCHITECT:	I have nothing to do with it. My problem is that whenever I try to design a green space, I can't.
SURVEYOR:	[*Moves about on all fours.*] Where is it?
ARCHITECT:	I haven't seen it yet. I'd like to see how it looks... I've just heard the noise it makes... So strange!
SURVEYOR:	How come?!
ARCHITECT:	I don't know exactly. But it is strange that a man is trying to destroy the foundations of the city with his bulldozer. [*Crumples up his drawing paper and tosses it into the garbage can.*] No... No... I can't. There isn't even an inch of land left for the green space.
SURVEYOR:	But there should be a green space.
ARCHITECT:	I can't do anything about it. I think the measurements are wrong.

SURVEYOR:	Do you mean that I've made a mistake?
ARCHITECT:	Maybe...
SURVEYOR:	Are you serious?
ARCHITECT:	Yes...
SURVEYOR:	Impossible... I never make mistakes.
ARCHITECT:	You always make mistakes just because you think you don't.
SURVEYOR:	What the hell do you want of me now?
ARCHITECT:	Nothing... There is enough noise here, just don't start shouting.
SURVEYOR:	[*Gently.*] You don't like loud noises, do you?
ARCHITECT:	Yeah... It takes my head off!
SURVEYOR:	Me too.
ARCHITECT:	No... It makes no difference to you.
SURVEYOR:	It does. But I just don't care about it.
ARCHITECT:	Oh, I can't do it. It's because of this noise.
SURVEYOR:	Don't care about it.
ARCHITECT:	I can't help it. Especially when this horrible noise is emptying the ground beneath me.
SURVEYOR:	The city needs sewers you know.
ARCHITECT:	I don't care. It is driving me mad.
SURVEYOR:	Sewers are needed to transport waste matter of the people...
ARCHITECT:	To live somewhere on the top of them! Is this what you mean?
SURVEYOR:	No way out. The city will be buried under the sewage if there is no sewage system.
ARCHITECT:	What's the use of it? In this way, the only thing which remains of man is their waste matter, either on or under the ground.

SURVEYOR:	I think, there is a big difference. The important thing is to keep the city clean.
ARCHITECT:	It's the humans who matter most and what they leave behind.
SURVEYOR:	What about you, yourself?
ARCHITECT:	Me?!
SURVEYOR:	Yeah, ... don't you leave shit?
ARCHITECT:	I do...
SURVEYOR:	I do too. Only dead people don't leave waste matter. Leaving shit means having life.
ARCHITECT:	O!
SURVEYOR:	No way out. You have to accept it.
ARCHITECT:	[*Draws a few lines.*] No... It is not right... [*Crumples up his drawing paper and tosses it into the garbage can.*] I must find some other way.
SURVEYOR:	For what?
ARCHITECT:	To design a green space.
SURVEYOR:	What about the waste matter?
ARCHITECT:	The waste matter?!
SURVEYOR:	Yeah... [*Picks up the theodolite and puts it down again carefully.*] The amount of shit left by everybody depends on the time during which he lives.
ARCHITECT:	So, what?
SURVEYOR:	I mean the longer you live, the more shit you leave. That way, you can tell a person's age by the amount of shit he's left. [*Moves about on all fours on the stage.*]

ARCHITECT:	[*Puts another drawing paper on the table while the* SURVEYOR *is talking.*] I must do the measurements correctly this time.
SURVEYOR:	[*Turns his face to the audience while on all fours.*] In fact, you can count the number of heads in a city by their shit. This way, the city population can be estimated too.
ARCHITECT:	[*Scrawls on the paper angrily.*] No room is left over there. The earth has a finite capacity, you know.
	[*The horrible sound of a collapsing building rolls over the stage. The* ARCHITECT *and* SURVEYOR *run away and take shelter in a corner. The noise of a working bulldozer is still heard.*]
ARCHITECT:	What was that?
SURVEYOR:	What was that?
ARCHITECT:	I think something collapsed.
SURVEYOR:	What?
ARCHITECT:	[*Keeps his head down and looks at the floor, horrified.*] Oh... Here... Beneath the floor...
SURVEYOR:	No, ... impossible!
ARCHITECT:	But yes. I think... the sewer's roof... has collapsed.
SURVEYOR:	But... why does the bulldozer still work?
ARCHITECT:	We should dig it out somehow.
SURVEYOR:	Nobody can do anything now. It's happened, what was supposed to. By the way, we don't know how to get under there either.
ARCHITECT:	It is all because of the people's waste matter. [*Puts his ear on the floor.*] There is nothing but this damn noise of the machine.

SURVEYOR:	I've found it at last. It was right here!
ARCHITECT:	[*Gets up hastily.*] What?!
SURVEYOR:	[*Holds up the spring before his eyes.*] I will never let it slip again.
ARCHITECT:	[*Sits on his chair behind the table feebly.*] What do you think is now going on under the ground?
SURVEYOR:	[*Busy repairing the theodolite.*] Where?!
ARCHITECT:	Under the ground... I asked you what's going on under here?
SURVEYOR:	[*Tries to fix the spring.*] Just a minute...
ARCHITECT:	I think all the bad smells of the world came together there.
SURVEYOR:	Ah!
ARCHITECT:	Are you disgusted?
SURVEYOR:	No... I am getting angry with it.
ARCHITECT:	To me, it is nauseous.
SURVEYOR:	This bloody spring is pestering me. I don't know why it won't fix?
ARCHITECT:	Can I help you?
SURVEYOR:	No, ... I can handle it myself.
ARCHITECT:	As you wish... I thought you might need some help.
SURVEYOR:	No... just be quiet and let me do my work.
ARCHITECT:	Am I a burden on you?
SURVEYOR:	No, but when you speak, it distracts my attention.
ARCHITECT:	Take it easy.
SURVEYOR:	I don't believe it. Wow!
ARCHITECT:	What happened?

SURVEYOR:	It slipped again. It is your fault.
ARCHITECT:	My fault?!
SURVEYOR:	[*Looks for the spring on all fours.*] Yeah… You talk too much.
ARCHITECT:	I am horrified.
SURVEYOR:	What the hell can I do for you? If you want, come and look for the spring.
ARCHITECT:	[*Gets busy drawing.*] No… Everything is mixed up… By the way …
SURVEYOR:	What?
ARCHITECT:	The bulldozer is still working under the ground.
SURVEYOR:	I can hear it.
ARCHITECT:	So, the driver must be alive.
SURVEYOR:	[*Draws a path on the ground with his finger.*] Yeah… I think he must be somewhere under here.
ARCHITECT:	[*Leaves his drawing board and sits down on the floor. Finds the spring and throws it away after playing with it… Then puts his ear on the floor and pauses for a moment.*] Stop moving around… I think I heard something. He is moving.
SURVEYOR:	Don't worry about him. He is all right.
ARCHITECT:	What if he's not? Maybe he's injured and the machine is working by itself?
SURVEYOR:	It doesn't matter.
ARCHITECT:	Yes, it does! It really matters. What if he is dead?
SURVEYOR:	No, he isn't.

ARCHITECT:	So, where did the collapsing sound come from?
SURVEYOR:	I think it was not too far.
ARCHITECT:	But we have to know where it was.
SURVEYOR:	That's just what we need! We will have to find it now, and rebuild it tomorrow.
ARCHITECT:	Now?!
SURVEYOR:	When then?
ARCHITECT:	Wait until tomorrow. Everywhere is dark now.
SURVEYOR:	Yeah... we can't see in this darkness.
ARCHITECT:	I wish the sound would stop by morning somehow.
SURVEYOR:	We have no other choice. You must accept that the bulldozer guarantees our comfort.
ARCHITECT:	Comfort?!
SURVEYOR:	If it stops working, we will all be sunk in our sewage. Because of this sound, the city is clean by now.
	The noise of the bulldozer stops.
ARCHITECT:	Ah... It's stopped. I've gotten rid of it at last!
SURVEYOR:	What? Has it stopped?
ARCHITECT:	Now, I can get down to my work in complete peace of mind.
SURVEYOR:	[*Desperate.*] He must have stopped to have a rest.
ARCHITECT:	How do you think he can see in the darkness?
SURVEYOR:	You are right... It must be too dark under there.

ARCHITECT: It must be dark wherever there is no window.

SURVEYOR: So, he must be very sharp-eyed.

ARCHITECT: Is it possible? What a strange guy!

SURVEYOR: I think it is impossible to work underground with ordinary eyes.

ARCHITECT: I'd like to meet him.

SURVEYOR: So, would I. But how can we find him?

ARCHITECT: He is under here, isn't he?

SURVEYOR: Right.

ARCHITECT: So, let's call him. [*Stamps his feet and runs toward the front of the stage.*] Hey! Do you hear us? [*Puts his ear on the floor.*] Nothing is heard.

SURVEYOR: I've found it. [*Picks up the spring and looks at it.*]

ARCHITECT: [*Turns to SURVEYOR.*] Where was it?

SURVEYOR: Just here... [*Takes the theodolite and resumes repairing it.*] It was just at my feet. I found it by accident.

ARCHITECT: There is no sound at all.

SURVEYOR: You were disturbed by the sound, weren't you?

ARCHITECT: But there's something wrong with this deep silence. It hurts me.

SURVEYOR: It doesn't make any difference, does it? Silence is silence anyway.

ARCHITECT: Maybe I'd better get busy with my work. [*Sits behind his drawing board and starts working. But can't concentrate and stops working.*] It doesn't work... I can't. Perhaps the weather is the problem. The more I try, the less I make progress. I think there is something wrong with it.

SURVEYOR: If I manage to fix the spring, it would be all right. That's the problem.

ARCHITECT: [*Gets up and moves around the stage.*] Nothing can be heard. As if... as if something dreadful is lurking behind this silence.

SURVEYOR: [*Tries to fix the spring.*] What, for example?

ARCHITECT: I don't exactly know... Maybe the roar of an explosion.

SURVEYOR: Please shut up!

ARCHITECT: I can't... I have to speak.

SURVEYOR: Ah... it slipped again.

ARCHITECT: Well, fasten it to your finger with a piece of string.

SURVEYOR: I will, if I find it... [*Crawls on the floor on all fours.*]

ARCHITECT: Maybe he is hurt, eh?

SURVEYOR: I don't think so. Maybe he is taking a rest.

ARCHITECT: But it's been a long time.

SURVEYOR: Is it possible...

ARCHITECT: ...that he's died underground?

SURVEYOR: Maybe...

ARCHITECT: In that case, we should dig him out.

SURVEYOR: But how? We have no tools.

ARCHITECT: Poor guy! He was buried alive under people's waste matter.

SURVEYOR: It's not clear yet.

ARCHITECT:	Why has the bulldozer stopped working then?
SURVEYOR:	He has probably fallen asleep.
ARCHITECT:	No... He laid down his life to clean the city, to clear the people's waste matter.
SURVEYOR:	What a great man!
ARCHITECT:	[*Punches the floor excitedly.*] Hey... Answer me if you are alive. Do you hear us?
SURVEYOR:	Be quiet.
ARCHITECT:	The damage is done! I think he is dead.
SURVEYOR:	[*Puts his finger on his nose to make the* ARCHITECT *keep quiet.*] Shush! [*Puts his ear on the floor.*] I think I heard something.
ARCHITECT:	Did he say something? [*Rushes to the* SURVEYOR *and puts his ear on the floor too.*] Hey guy... You... Say that you are alive.
SURVEYOR:	Shush! I told you to be quiet. Ah... Do you hear a thud too?
ARCHITECT:	Yeah... So, he is still alive.
SURVEYOR:	It stopped.
	[A YOUNG MAN *enters.*]
MAN:	Excuse me sir...
ARCHITECT:	His voice... I heard his voice. He said excuse me.
SURVEYOR:	I heard him too. Hi!
MAN:	Sorry... I...
	[*The* SURVEYOR *and* ARCHITECT *notice him.*]
ARCHITECT:	Well, you are here, aren't you?
MAN:	Yes, ... I've already arrived.
SURVEYOR:	How wonderful!

MAN:	Did you know that I was coming?
ARCHITECT:	Honestly, ... we thought you were dead.
MAN:	Me?! Why?
SURVEYOR:	Never mind... Don't worry. Glad to see that you're quite well.
MAN:	Thank you. That's very kind of you, but...
SURVEYOR:	Why don't you come in? [*Accompanies him.*] Please come in.
MAN:	Thank you...
ARCHITECT:	Are you sure you are all right?
MAN:	No... Yes... I'm just a little tired.
SURVEYOR:	You had a break, didn't you?
MAN:	Break?! No. How can I have a rest in such confusion?
ARCHITECT:	Yes. It is impossible to take a nap with all that noise. We were nearly going mad in here.
MAN:	As a matter of fact, there was no noise, but...
ARCHITECT:	But it was so loud, particularly in a closed place.
MAN:	No. I heard nothing.
SURVEYOR:	Maybe you've got used to it.
MAN:	Got used to it?! To what?
SURVEYOR:	To the noise...
MAN:	I got used to nothing. I don't like noises at all.
ARCHITECT:	Maybe there is something wrong with your ears!
MAN:	As a matter of fact, they are very healthy.
SURVEYOR:	Your eyes... What about your eyes?
MAN:	[*Rubs his eyes.*] Well... my eyes...

SURVEYOR:	I mean they must be too sharp.
ARCHITECT:	If you were late, we would have searched for you.
MAN:	Searched for me?!
ARCHITECT:	Right... But it is good that you've come on your own.
MAN:	Spare my blushes.
SURVEYOR:	So, would you please do me a favor?
MAN:	Just as you say, whatever it is.
SURVEYOR:	Please find the spring for me.
MAN:	The spring?!
SURVEYOR:	Yes. I lost it. I'm sure you can find it in a twinkling of an eye.
MAN:	Me?! How come you think so?
SURVEYOR:	It is a tiny spring. I think it must be somewhere over there.
MAN:	Well... [Looks around.] It is somehow dark here.
SURVEYOR:	Then how could you see there? In the darkness?
MAN:	The moon is out.
ARCHITECT:	Impossible... Do you mean the moon was out over there?
MAN:	Yes. Why should I lie to you?
ARCHITECT:	[Whispers to the SURVEYOR.] He is babbling nonsense. As if he's been disturbed by the loud noise.
SURVEYOR:	[Looks at the YOUNG MAN from the corner of his eyes.] No... he is fully alert. He's trying to dodge work. [Turns to the YOUNG MAN.] Did you say the moon was out there?

MAN:	Yes…
SURVEYOR:	Do you think I am a fool? You are a fool! [*Shouts.*] How come the moon was out even under the ground?
MAN:	It's not my fault that the moon is out tonight.
SURVEYOR:	I'll teach you a lesson. [*Takes hold of the MAN and throws him on the floor.*] Hurry up. Start looking for it.
MAN:	For what?
SURVEYOR:	I told you to find the spring.
MAN:	[*Submissively.*] Alright. I will. [*Takes his glasses out of his pocket and puts them on.*] I can see better this way.
SURVEYOR:	Well, you wear glasses, don't you?
MAN:	[*Takes his glasses off hastily.*] No… No… It is not necessary.
ARCHITECT:	[*Approaches the* SURVEYOR.] Calm down. Be nice to him.
MAN:	[*Crawls on the floor on all fours.*] But I don't know where it is.
ARCHITECT:	[*Goes to the* YOUNG MAN *and sits on his knees.*] Don't take it to heart. He has a strange temper and is a little impetuous but he is kind as well. [*Points in a direction.*] Maybe it's over there.
MAN:	I looked. It wasn't there.
SURVEYOR:	Why didn't you answer our shouts?
ARCHITECT:	From now on, we make an arrangement. Whenever you hear us calling, blow the horn a few times.
MAN:	For what?

SURVEYOR:	To see if you are still alive.
MAN:	Is it important to you?
ARCHITECT:	Of course, it is. If you blow the horn, we will be sure that you are still alive.
MAN:	But how? I haven't got a horn.
SURVEYOR:	We know. I mean blow the bulldozer's horn.
MAN:	[*Puzzled.*] Bulldozer?
ARCHITECT:	It has got a horn, hasn't it?
MAN:	I don't really know! What bulldozer?
SURVEYOR:	The one you drive!
ARCHITECT:	Hey... you are the bulldozer driver, aren't you?
MAN:	Me? I don't know how to drive at all.
ARCHITECT:	Well, who drives it then?
MAN:	I don't know. How should I know?
ARCHITECT:	You were there, I mean under the ground, weren't you?
MAN:	No! I was just looking for my house.
ARCHITECT:	[*Gets up and goes to the* SURVEYOR *hurriedly.*] We have mistaken him for the bulldozer driver.
SURVEYOR:	I see...
ARCHITECT:	So, apologize to him quickly.
SURVEYOR:	What shall I do?
ARCHITECT:	Soothe him.
SURVEYOR:	[*Goes toward the* YOUNG MAN *and helps him kindly to stand up.*] Sorry... Sir... Please get up and come with me. [*Sits him on a chair.*] Forgive me sir, I treated you badly. In fact, I had mistaken you for someone else.

MAN:	Never mind. You must be tired. I didn't mean to bother you but I had to… I'm looking for an address.
ARCHITECT:	I knew… [*Goes to a corner.*] I knew that he was dead.
SURVEYOR:	What can we do for you, now?
MAN:	I have lost my way.
SURVEYOR:	Are you lost?! Where do you want to go?
MAN:	My home… I am looking for my home. I couldn't find it.
SURVEYOR:	What is your house's address?
MAN:	I don't know, but I think it must be somewhere near here!
SURVEYOR:	You must be tired.
MAN:	Yes… I am. I looked everywhere. There was nobody to help me… I am so tired.
ARCHITECT:	[*Approaches the* SURVEYOR *and whispers.*] I think it is not advisable to let a stranger come into our room.
SURVEYOR:	But he has lost his way home.
ARCHITECT:	I don't care who he is. We don't know him. I think we'd better entertain him in the office.
SURVEYOR:	I didn't mean to take him into our bedroom.
MAN:	I am sorry. I didn't mean to cause you any trouble.
SURVEYOR:	No, … it is no trouble at all. Please relax.
MAN:	The city is too crowded.
SURVEYOR:	Yes…
ARCHITECT:	There isn't even an inch of land left for the green space.

MAN:	Building! Everywhere is building! You lose your own home among all these buildings… It is so strange.
ARCHITECT:	[*Sits down, punches the floor several times, and pauses.*] No… I can't hear anything.
SURVEYOR:	Stand up! Can't you see we have a guest?
ARCHITECT:	What a helpless man!
MAN:	[*Ashamed.*] If I was not helpless, I would not be wandering about late at night.
SURVEYOR:	Don't be insulted, he didn't mean you.
ARCHITECT:	[*Gets closer to the floor.*] Hey, sir! Do you hear me?
MAN:	[*Astonished.*] Excuse me, who is he talking to?
SURVEYOR:	To a helpless man whose voice we could hear just a few minutes ago.
MAN:	But he is talking to the floor!
SURVEYOR:	No, he is talking to the man who is trapped under the floor. If he is still alive, of course.
MAN:	Where?
SURVEYOR:	[*Points to the floor.*] Just here. Under the ground.
ARCHITECT:	He is dead. Nobody helped him. He is buried alive.
MAN:	[*Horrified.*] What? Buried alive? Under here? [*Jumps up.*]
ARCHITECT:	Yes. We are sure he was alive a few minutes ago but now only God knows.
MAN:	[*Goes forward and looks at the floor.*] How do you know?
ARCHITECT:	He was working on his bulldozer.

MAN:	[*Looks at them, horrified.*] On... on his bulldozer?!
ARCHITECT:	Yes, he was buried alive with his bulldozer.
MAN:	[*Looks at them hesitatingly, then a bewildered smile appears on his face.*] You... It is impossible!
ARCHITECT:	Yes... At first, we thought he had turned off his engine to have a rest, but it took a long time and we aren't so sure.
MAN:	Well... I... I don't think...
SURVEYOR:	That's right. A break wouldn't be so long.
ARCHITECT:	Then we came to the conclusion that he's dead!
MAN:	Who buried him alive?
SURVEYOR:	But I'm not sure that he is dead!
ARCHITECT:	I am quite sure that he is.
SURVEYOR:	I think... he might have fallen asleep... Yes, he has fallen asleep. First, he had a cup of tea. Then he decided to light a cigarette and take a nap.
MAN:	[*Gets up, frightened.*] Sorry sirs. I think I had better leave. As if...
SURVEYOR:	Stay still! [*Takes a step forward.*] Stay still, or the spring will slip again.
MAN:	[*Cowers a bit.*] Yes!
SURVEYOR:	Watch the spring... Don't move. Stay still... [*Goes forward to the* YOUNG MAN *slowly. As if he is trying to catch an insect, bends near the* YOUNG MAN, *catches the spring from the floor, and lets out a loud shout at the same time.*]

MAN:	[*Shouts and jumps back.*] What happened?
SURVEYOR:	I've found it. I will never let it slip again. I will fix it now.
ARCHITECT:	You'd better throw your theodolite away!
SURVEYOR:	My theodolite?!
ARCHITECT:	I think it is worn out and of no use anymore.
SURVEYOR:	What about you... with all those wrong plans?
ARCHITECT:	It is because of your theodolite. It does not function properly and shows anything erroneous.
SURVEYOR:	If I can fix the spring, it will be right. [*Starts repairing the theodolite.*]
ARCHITECT:	So, be careful.
SURVEYOR:	I caught it...
ARCHITECT:	Fasten it to your finger by a piece of string.
SURVEYOR:	Where the hell can I find a piece of string, now? [*Tries his best to fix the spring.*]
MAN:	I am very sorry to hear that a man is buried alive with his bulldozer.
ARCHITECT:	Yes. His devotion will live forever, although we couldn't see him. He died for us.
MAN:	[*Depressed.*] What a noble man!
SURVEYOR:	For me and you... to keep the earth clean... [*Points to the floor.*] Now he is dead. He's dead under here. But we are not sure yet!
ARCHITECT:	[*To the* YOUNG MAN.] A devoted man who died for us. May he rest in peace. [*Approaches the* YOUNG MAN.] A great man who died alone and helpless, and nobody

	heard his cries too. Now, he is under your feet.
MAN:	[*Goes hurriedly to the other side of the stage.*] Under my feet?! But ... But there's no trace of digging here.
ARCHITECT:	That is the problem. If we knew how he got there, we could have saved him.
MAN:	[*Laughs, frightened.*] You... You are kidding me.
ARCHITECT:	[*Stands face to face with the* YOUNG MAN.] Look at me carefully. Have you seen me before?
MAN:	[*Tries to step back.*] No... No... I haven't.
ARCHITECT:	So, there is no reason for kidding.
SURVEYOR:	Well-done! I fixed it at last.
ARCHITECT:	[*Looks at the floor regretfully.*] What a pity!
	[*The* SURVEYOR *puts down his theodolite gently, goes to the other side of the stage, and brings three cups of tea.*]
SURVEYOR:	We'd better drink a cup of tea to get refreshed. Don't worry, we will soon know what has really happened under there.
MAN:	Thank you very much, but I must go home.
ARCHITECT:	You can't leave in this darkness. You will get lost.
MAN:	I am lost already. But I have to go. I have nowhere to go but my home.
ARCHITECT:	[*Drinks his tea.*] Nowhere?
MAN:	I have lived in this city for ages, but... But I don't know why I lose my way home these days.

SURVEYOR:	[*Drinks his tea.*] Have you lost your way before?
MAN:	Yes, but I could usually find it at last. I don't know why I couldn't find it tonight.
ARCHITECT:	Did you search well?
MAN:	Yes. I went the same way as usual.
SURVEYOR:	Maybe there is something wrong with your eyes.
ARCHITECT:	You should have asked for help.
MAN:	There was nobody. I was lucky to find you.
SURVEYOR:	Are you happy now?
MAN:	Happy?
ARCHITECT:	Happy to find us.
MAN:	Yes, but it would be better if I were in my own house.
SURVEYOR:	Ah!... Damn it!... It slipped again!
MAN:	[*Turns back, surprised.*] What?
ARCHITECT:	I think it wouldn't be called a theodolite anymore!
SURVEYOR:	But it must be. We have plenty of work tomorrow.
ARCHITECT:	I don't care. What is the point? ... Are you worried about the city which is hollow underneath?
SURVEYOR:	What is happening under the ground doesn't concern me. I must complete the plan of the city.
ARCHITECT:	I can no longer do it. It is important for me to know where I am standing. I wouldn't like to stay at a place which is hollow underneath.

SURVEYOR:	[*Follows the direction which he thinks the spring would have slipped.*] I have to do my duty anyway. What will happen next does not concern me.
MAN:	[*To the* SURVEYOR.] I think the spring slipped over there.
SURVEYOR:	No sir, I don't think so.
MAN:	It is there anyway.
SURVEYOR:	I don't need your help. If you had a sense of direction, you wouldn't have lost your way.
MAN:	Excuse me. I only wanted...
SURVEYOR:	Don't apologize. Why don't you go home?
MAN:	I have lost my way.
SURVEYOR:	I know that. Go and find it.
MAN:	I went. But I couldn't find it. I came here to ask you for help.
SURVEYOR:	Why didn't you say that earlier?
MAN:	I wanted to. But one word leads to another.
SURVEYOR:	We have the map of this city point by point.
MAN:	Even my home?!
SURVEYOR:	Yeah... If I find it, I will fasten it to my finger.
MAN:	Very well. So, I will come here every night to ask you for help.
ARCHITECT:	[*Stops working.*] What if you can't find your way here?
SURVEYOR:	[*Looks for something on the floor.*] No... As if it's gone to the ground.
MAN:	I don't know.
ARCHITECT:	Something should be done.
MAN:	What, for example?

ARCHITECT:	Many people lose their way home nowadays.
SURVEYOR:	If I can find it this time...
ARCHITECT:	As long as that screw is lost your spring will not be fixed.
MAN:	I must mark my way from home to work.
SURVEYOR:	What a good idea.
ARCHITECT:	What if everybody does it?
SURVEYOR:	Then, there would be a helter-skelter situation in the city. Everybody would end up in a wrong house... I think the spring must be over there. [*Points in a direction and walks there.*] Damn it... As if it's vanished.
MAN:	Please find it for me anyway.
ARCHITECT:	But how? Give me your address.
MAN:	There it is. [*Gives a piece of paper to the ARCHITECT.*] 79th floor, Building #803214, 547 Street.
SURVEYOR:	How straight! How big is your house?
MAN:	About 20 square meters in area.
ARCHITECT:	Just a moment. I will find it.
MAN:	Thank you very much.
SURVEYOR:	Don't worry. The whole map of the city is in our hands. We'll find anywhere you want immediately. [*Looks for the spring on all fours.*]
MAN:	Yes...
ARCHITECT:	Ah... I found it.
SURVEYOR:	[*Still looking for the spring.*] Impossible.
ARCHITECT:	No... It's not the spring!
MAN:	Perhaps my house is not on your map.

ARCHITECT:	Of course, it is.
MAN:	You know... I feel peace only in my own house. If I lose it, I will be wandering forever, or I may die.
ARCHITECT:	Everybody should have a place to live in. I mean a secure place.
MAN:	That's right.
SURVEYOR:	[*Moves on all fours.*] Where is it?
MAN:	[*Points in a direction.*] Over there...
SURVEYOR:	[*Without looking at the* YOUNG MAN.] It is impossible! It should be over here. [*Rubs his hand on the ground.*]
ARCHITECT:	I am afraid I can't find it.
MAN:	[*Embarrassed.*] Couldn't you find it?
ARCHITECT:	At least not on this map. I must look for it on the other maps.
MAN:	I have caused you so much trouble.
ARCHITECT:	Do you think you can find your house in this darkness?
MAN:	I'll try to.
SURVEYOR:	I would find it, if there were lighter here. [*Rubs his hand on the floor.*]
ARCHITECT:	But I think you can't find it in this situation.
MAN:	Don't say it... Help me, please.
ARCHITECT:	Just a moment... I will do my best and you must be careful not to get lost like all the people who have lost themselves among the slabs of concrete.
MAN:	Where?
ARCHITECT:	In this concrete forest which has grown out of land. Everybody in this city lives within the

hollow trunks of these concrete trees which have no roots. Their foundations are empty. There are lots of sewers to carry off the people's waste matter, but there aren't enough yet.

SURVEYOR: I have to keep on searching...

MAN: Who has made this city?

ARCHITECT: The city is in danger of collapse. We have to prepare a new map for the city.

SURVEYOR: So, we can find an unoccupied place to plant one of those concrete trees in it.

MAN: But what about my house?

SURVEYOR: Be quiet...

MAN: Please help me.

ARCHITECT: Shall I help you get hidden among the slabs of concrete?

MAN: Get hidden?!... From whom?

ARCHITECT: From each other... From yourself...

SURVEYOR: I asked you to be quiet! You are distracting me. [*Still moves on all fours.*]

MAN: Why should I hide myself? I have done nothing wrong.

ARCHITECT: If you are innocent, why do you feel comfortable among all those slabs of concrete?

MAN: No... I have committed no sin!

ARCHITECT: But you have. All of you are sinners.

MAN: Please... please find the way to my house.

SURVEYOR: [*Crouching down, hopeless.*] There is no sign of it.

ARCHITECT:	[*Puts aside another map.*] It's not here, either.
SURVEYOR:	[*Starts searching.*] It must be found.
MAN:	Give it a second try... It'll be found. Maybe you were wrong.
ARCHITECT:	No, I wasn't. I know why they hide themselves among the slabs of concrete.
SURVEYOR:	Why can't I do it?
ARCHITECT:	[*To the* YOUNG MAN.] Do you know why? Do you know why they hide themselves among the slabs of concrete? Because they leave too much shit! That's why they have caused so much trouble for themselves and for the others.
MAN:	That's right. The people's waste matter is increasing.
ARCHITECT:	And it is increasing day by day... Ah... I found it at last.
SURVEYOR:	[*Crawling backward on all fours.*] No, I didn't.
MAN:	Thank you... [*Tries to see the map.*] I knew... I knew my house would never get lost.
SURVEYOR:	[*Lies on the ground and leans his chin against his hands.*] I think I have lost it forever.
ARCHITECT:	[*Pushes the* YOUNG MAN *back.*] Get out, let me see!
MAN:	Thank you! Is my house too far from here?
ARCHITECT:	[*Gets up and points in a direction.*] You must go straight that way, then turn to the right, keep on going, there is another turn in the road, again turn right, there you will find an 84-story building. That's your house!
MAN:	That's it! Thank you.

[*The noise of the bulldozer is heard again.*]

SURVEYOR:	[*Startles.*] He is alive!
ARCHITECT:	He is not dead! There it is, the noise again! [*Rushes to the center of the stage, sits down, and speaks to the floor.*] Hey! You are still alive, aren't you?
SURVEYOR:	We are glad to hear you again!
ARCHITECT:	No, I am not glad!
SURVEYOR:	Why?
ARCHITECT:	Because he is hollowing out the ground underneath us, now.
SURVEYOR:	I think you have forgotten the problem of the waste matter.
ARCHITECT:	And because of it we must be ready for everything.
SURVEYOR:	[*To the* YOUNG MAN.] Do you hear it? He is digging a sewer for you.
ARCHITECT:	To save you from drowning in your own waste matter.
MAN:	Who is he?
SURVEYOR:	Who!... He?
ARCHITECT:	He is the man we thought was buried alive.
SURVEYOR:	Now, the sound shows that life is going on there.
ARCHITECT:	This sound... This sound is the sound of death...
SURVEYOR:	Listen how loud it is! Don't say that it bothers you.
ARCHITECT:	No, it scares me.
MAN:	I see something is going on here. [*Goes back.*]

SURVEYOR:	No. It is the symbol of life and power.
ARCHITECT:	He is like a mole.
SURVEYOR:	A mole?
ARCHITECT:	Yes, a mole.
	[*The* YOUNG MAN *exits.*]
SURVEYOR:	No. He can't be a mole.
ARCHITECT:	How do you know that? You have seen seen him, haven't you?
SURVEYOR:	No... But I know a mole can't drive a bulldozer!
ARCHITECT:	So, what is it?
SURVEYOR:	What? It...
ARCHITECT:	It is a giant mole which is destroying the foundation of the city.
SURVEYOR:	[*Notices that the* YOUNG MAN *is not there.*] He is gone!
ARCHITECT:	What?
SURVEYOR:	The man... he is gone.
ARCHITECT:	It's as if nobody was here. It was just a dream.
SURVEYOR:	It was not a dream. He was really here.
ARCHITECT:	He had lost his way. Did you see him come?
SURVEYOR:	Yeah...
ARCHITECT:	But none of us saw his departure. [*Counts the cups of tea.*] There are three cups here.
SURVEYOR:	It means there must have been another person here.
ARCHITECT:	Not definitely.
SURVEYOR:	But we saw him come, didn't we?

ARCHITECT:	Look… Two of cups are empty and the third is untouched. So, nobody has been here!
SURVEYOR:	Maybe he was here but he didn't drink it.
ARCHITECT:	I am beginning to suspect everything, even our existence!
SURVEYOR:	[*Horrified.*] You mean that we do not exist?
ARCHITECT:	Why are we here, after all?
SURVEYOR:	Look… Please don't say these things… I am afraid.
ARCHITECT:	Afraid of what?
SURVEYOR:	Of your words. You speak so strangely!
ARCHITECT:	Which is stranger, my words or our work?
	[*The bulldozer stops working.*]
SURVEYOR:	It has stopped again!
ARCHITECT:	Everything is too strange here. I feel I am getting crushed under a thousand cold eyes!
SURVEYOR:	Be quiet!
ARCHITECT:	We are being buried under the cold glares. Look! [*Grabs the SURVEYOR's hand, shows him around the stage, and points in different directions.*] Look! Do you see all those eyes?
	[A tall and thin BLIND MAN *enters. He is wearing dark glasses and a long dusty black garment covers his body. He brings an unpleasant odor onto the stage.*]
SURVEYOR:	No… I don't want to see.
ARCHITECT:	You must see.
SURVEYOR:	I can't… [*Releases himself from the ARCHITECT's hand, walks backward, and hits the* BLIND MAN. *He gives a loud shout and pulls himself away.*] What a horrible smell!

BLIND MAN:	How terrifying it was!
SURVEYOR:	[*Cleans himself with his trembling hands.*] Who are you?
BLIND MAN:	So, you are here! [*Moves to the center of the stage.*]
ARCHITECT:	[*Covers his nose with his hand.*] Who are you?
BLIND MAN:	…
SURVEYOR:	What do you want?
ARCHITECT:	Have you lost your way?
BLIND MAN:	…
SURVEYOR:	If you have lost your way too, we can help you find it.
BLIND MAN:	…
ARCHITECT:	Do you hear us?
BLIND MAN:	Why did you stop working?… [*Sits on a chair, imperiously.*]
SURVEYOR:	My theodolite's spring…
BLIND MAN:	You don't need it anymore!
SURVEYOR:	[*Takes a few steps toward him.*] But my work is not finished yet.
BLIND MAN:	Don't approach me… Keep your distance… Your work is finished. My work is finished, too.
ARCHITECT:	Who are you?
BLIND MAN:	How come you don't know me? I am your neighbor! [*Points to the ground.*] I was under here.
SURVEYOR:	So, you are the bulldozer driver, aren't you? I am the Surveyor…

BLIND MAN:	I know who you are. Keep away from each other.
SURVEYOR:	You heard our shouting, didn't you? You don't know how happy we were when we realized you hadn't died.
BLIND MAN:	Died?!
ARCHITECT:	Yes... We thought you were dead.
SURVEYOR:	But I knew you were alive and turned off the bulldozer just to take a rest.
BLIND MAN:	No... I went to have a look around at that time.
ARCHITECT:	Is there anything interesting to see under the ground?
BLIND MAN:	The whole underneath of the city is hollow. Tell me if it's day or night.
ARCHITECT:	You can see yourself.
BLIND MAN:	[*Imperiously.*] I asked if it's day or night.
ARCHITECT:	It is night. So, your eyes...
BLIND MAN:	I don't need them. It is too dark under the ground. Yeah, I am blind. What did you think? [*Laughs loudly.*] But I did something wonderful with my bulldozer. There was no place left. By the way, is there anybody else here besides us?
SURVEYOR:	No. Everybody is sleeping in their own house this time at night.
BLIND MAN:	Poor guys! No, there is someone else here!
ARCHITECT:	You can't see. What are you talking about!
BLIND MAN:	Someone is nearby here.
	[*A terrible sound is heard. The* ARCHITECT *and* SURVEYOR *rush to the corner and take*

shelter. The BLIND MAN *is sitting, careless and indifferent.*]

BLIND MAN:	Another one!
ARCHITECT:	What?
BLIND MAN:	You should come under the ground and see with your own eyes. It is worth seeing. What a pity! What a pity that I am not there now.
SURVEYOR:	But you are blind. How can you see?
BLIND MAN:	I told you... You don't need eyes under the ground.
ARCHITECT:	What's going on there?
BLIND MAN:	Nothing! It is just hollow. [*Laughs.*] I am finished with my work. Our number is up. We are not safe here. Be careful when you are walking, otherwise the ground under your feet will collapse.
ARCHITECT:	[*Tiptoes to a safe place with great horror.*] I... I knew it would end up like this.
BLIND MAN:	Don't try to escape. There's nowhere to go.
SURVEYOR:	[*Runs to the other side of the stage.*] I found it...
ARCHITECT:	Are you crazy? Can't you walk slowly?
SURVEYOR:	[*Bends down and picks up something from the floor.*] No... It is not the spring... [*Notices the* ARCHITECT.] Did you say something?
ARCHITECT:	Yeah... Try to walk slowly.
BLIND MAN:	Everywhere will collapse inevitably... I know there is someone else here.
SURVEYOR:	Who can see?... We or you?
BLIND MAN:	Sight is a useless thing. It deceives you.
SURVEYOR:	I thought...

ARCHITECT:	Of course, for you…
BLIND MAN:	When everywhere is dark, sight is useless.
SURVEYOR:	Do you think everywhere is like under the ground?
BLIND MAN:	Everywhere will soon collapse underground… into the waste matter… It's dark under there…
ARCHITECT:	Even us?
BLIND MAN:	Nothing will remain on the land … The ground under your feet is empty, too! [*Laughs loudly.*]
ARCHITECT:	No! [*Gets mad at the* BLIND MAN's *protracted laughter and attacks him.*] Shut up! [*Grabs the* BLIND MAN *by the collar and lifts him up. The* BLIND MAN *is still laughing.*] I told you to shut up…
SURVEYOR:	[*Tries to separate them.*] Leave him alone! Come here…
BLIND MAN:	[*Laughing.*] Our number is up…
	[*A terrible sound rolls into the stage. The* ARCHITECT *takes his hands off the* BLIND MAN's *collar.*]
ARCHITECT:	Something collapsed!
BLIND MAN:	You should go down here to have a look!
SURVEYOR:	No!
BLIND MAN:	Your time is going to come soon.
ARCHITECT:	We should warn everybody!
BLIND MAN:	It's too late, now.
	[*At this moment, a* YOUNG WOMAN *with a baby in her arms rushes to the stage.*]
WOMAN:	Where is?

ARCHITECT:	What are you looking for?
WOMAN:	Home! [*Sits on the ground while holding her baby tightly in her arms.*] Sleep my boy... You can't sleep in your cradle again...
ARCHITECT:	Where's your home? Let me find it for you.
WOMAN:	Home?! [*Caresses the baby.*] Don't worry... Sleep my boy.
SURVEYOR:	Maybe she is ...
ARCHITECT:	[*Tries to console the* YOUNG WOMAN.] Don't worry... [*Approaches the* SURVEYOR.] We should help her.
SURVEYOR:	But how?
ARCHITECT:	She mustn't stay here.
SURVEYOR:	Where shall we take her? Nowhere is safe! [*The sound of another collapsing building rolls into the stage. The horrified woman cowers and holds the baby more tightly in her arms.*]
BLIND MAN:	It will go on until morning.
ARCHITECT:	Shut up, your big mole! It is all your fault.
BLIND MAN:	My fault? I just drove the bulldozer. Someone else is to blame. The one who controls all of us. You are to blame, too. I made the sewer with your plans.
SURVEYOR:	You are a liar.
BLIND MAN:	No... We have been working under the supervision of only one person.
ARCHITECT:	Who?
BLIND MAN:	Under there, you can learn a lot. A Blind Man like me is always making use of his ears. Tell that woman that she mustn't wait here. The

ground under her feet will collapse at any moment.

ARCHITECT: Leave here, lady… Don't stay here…

WOMAN: Aren't you going to help me?

SURVEYOR: We? We can't.

ARCHITECT: Take your baby and leave here… Maybe you can find somewhere clean.

WOMAN: Do you think I may find a place in which my baby will be safe?

ARCHITECT: I don't know…

BLIND MAN: There may be just one place…

ARCHITECT: Where? [*Rummages through his plans.*]

BLIND MAN: I don't know… We must wait here.

SURVEYOR: Wait for whom?

BLIND MAN: That Person who is in charge of all this!

ARCHITECT: Where is That Person?

BLIND MAN: I don't know. I came across That Person under the ground, but I don't know where about That Person is up here!

SURVEYOR: How will we know That Person?

BLIND MAN: Who?

SURVEYOR: That Person who is in charge of all this.

BLIND MAN: I don't know. But That Person is supposed to come here when we have finished our work.

ARCHITECT: [*Throws away his maps.*] No! There isn't any place!

BLIND MAN: Maybe not…

ARCHITECT: How come?… Where is it?

BLIND MAN: I don't know. I did my utmost, but I couldn't destroy its foundations.

ARCHITECT:	[*To the* YOUNG WOMAN.] You should go and find that place.
	[*The sound of another collapsing building rolls into the stage. The* ARCHITECT *and* SURVEYOR *take shelter at a corner of the stage. The* YOUNG WOMAN *looks around, horrified. The* BLIND MAN *is sitting indifferently.*]
BLIND MAN:	Another one...
WOMAN:	Very soon, the city will vanish off the face of the earth. And then the earth will tell its tales.
SURVEYOR:	[*Goes slowly toward the* YOUNG WOMAN. *Then stops and turns to the* ARCHITECT.] What did she say?
WOMAN:	[*Tidies up the blanket wrapped around her baby.*] Sleep my innocent sweetheart... Sleep... Sleep till morning... You know nothing about what will happen tonight.
SURVEYOR:	She is speaking in delirium.
BLIND MAN:	I don't know what she says, but it is not delirium.
ARCHITECT:	We should help her...
BLIND MAN:	Nobody can help her in this darkness.
	[*A babble is heard in the stage while some men and women are speaking. The* ARCHITECT *follows the tumult off stage.*]
BLIND MAN:	Where did he go?
SURVEYOR:	This tumult...
BLIND MAN:	It's the common hubbub of the city.
	[*The* ARCHITECT *returns hastily.*]

ARCHITECT:	Everybody is running away...
SURVEYOR:	How long should we wait?
BLIND MAN:	Until That Person arrives.
ARCHITECT:	I can't wait. I must go.
BLIND MAN:	You have no other place to go unless That Person arrives and shows you the way.
	[*The sound of some collapsing buildings is heard.*]
BLIND MAN:	Two other buildings...
SURVEYOR:	Shut up...
BLIND MAN:	Okay. But what about these sounds?
WOMAN:	[*Gets up and goes slowly to the end of the stage.*] We are lonely strangers in this city. We should travel together. [*Exits.*]
ARCHITECT:	Ridiculous!
SURVEYOR:	Did you say ridiculous?
ARCHITECT:	Yeah... It was ridiculous that I was trying to design a green space on land which was empty.
SURVEYOR:	The spring... The theodolite's spring.
ARCHITECT:	The earth couldn't hold that much waste matter inside. It was us who polluted the earth and now we must pay for it. We must atone for our sin.
	[*The sound of several collapsing buildings is heard.*]
BLIND MAN:	I couldn't count them this time.
SURVEYOR:	[*Looks at the floor.*] Where is it?
BLIND MAN:	It is of no use anymore.

ARCHITECT:	[*No sound is heard*] I think everybody has left the city.
BLIND MAN:	Only we have remained.
ARCHITECT:	[*To the* BLIND MAN.] Do you think the woman can be saved?
BLIND MAN:	If she could find a safe place, of course.
SURVEYOR:	Ah... Why can't I find it? [*Searches the floor.*]
ARCHITECT:	How can we find that place?
BLIND MAN:	I don't know...
SURVEYOR:	[*Still looking for the spring.*] It must be somewhere near here, but I don't know why I can't see it.
BLIND MAN:	Forget about it. Save yourself!
ARCHITECT:	I don't care anymore. Maybe I have no right to save myself.
SURVEYOR:	No. I'm tired. [*Squats on the floor.*] When will I find that bloody thing?
BLIND MAN:	Very soon.
ARCHITECT:	I don't want to see That Person.
BLIND MAN:	But That Person has always been here ordering us.
SURVEYOR:	[*Takes the theodolite and examines it carefully.*] How come?
ARCHITECT:	But we were unaware of That Person's presence. That Person has always misused us anyway. You were quite right. We have always been in hands of That Person like puppets. We were so immersed in our business that we even forgot ourselves.
BLIND MAN:	You will see That Person tonight.

[*The sound of another collapsing building is heard. The* ARCHITECT, *horrified, goes to a chair, crouches on it, and stares at the floor. The* SURVEYOR *and* BLIND MAN *show no reaction. After a few seconds, the sound of some more collapsing buildings is heard. Trying to keep off the ground, the* ARCHITECT *cowers much more tightly.*]

BLIND MAN: You can no longer keep count of them... It means That Person is approaching.

ARCHITECT: Seemed the sound source was close.

SURVEYOR: [*Crawls on the ground for a while, but can't find the spring. Returns and sits on his seat.*] It is not here!

BLIND MAN: It will be our turn very soon.

[*The* YOUNG MAN *enters with a sad, disappointed, sick smile on his face.*]

MAN: [*Choked back tears.*] I found it! [*Goes to the* ARCHITECT.] Thank you... The address you showed me was quite right. [*With split words.*] Thank you.

ARCHITECT: [*Horrified.*] No!

MAN: Yes, my house was safe.

ARCHITECT: [*Crying with horror.*] No... Poor guy... Your house is ruined.

MAN: [*Puts his finger on his nose.*] Shush! Don't say anything...

SURVEYOR: [*Looks around searching.*] It must be somewhere nearby.

BLIND MAN: You must keep on searching...

ARCHITECT: [*To the* YOUNG MAN.] Leave here...

MAN:	No… [*Kneels down and sits.*] Where should I go?
ARCHITECT:	Don't stay here… The ground is not safe.
MAN:	[*To himself.*] Where shall I go?
ARCHITECT:	There was a mother with her baby here. They went to find somewhere safe.
MAN:	Where did they go?
WOMAN:	[*Calling from far, off-stage.*] Is there any one to help me?
MAN:	Her cries!
SURVEYOR:	[*Looks for the spring without any attention to the others.*] No! It is not on the ground… I must look for it somewhere else.
WOMAN:	[*From far but another direction, off-stage.*] Is there any one to help me?
MAN:	[*Smiles.*] No…
	[*The YOUNG MAN gets up hurriedly and exits.*]
BLIND MAN:	That Person is about to come.
WOMAN:	[*Calling from far, off-stage.*] Is there any one to help me?
ARCHITECT:	[*Gets off the chair carefully and looks off stage.*] The woman's cries will go on all night. What a resurrection!
SURVEYOR:	[*Still looking for the spring.*] I should have known from the very beginning that this would be the result of carelessness.
	[*The sound of some collapsing buildings is heard. The sound is so near that even the BLIND MAN is shocked. The ARCHITECT*

begins to run about and the SURVEYOR *gets up.*]

BLIND MAN: We're in for it. It's approaching us!

ARCHITECT: It is disgusting...

BLIND MAN: That Person is about to appear!

SURVEYOR: [*Searching the floor, disappointed.*] What if I can't find it?

BLIND MAN: Don't worry, That Person will come to save us.

WOMAN: [*Calling from far and another direction, off-stage.*] Is there any one to help me?

ARCHITECT: She is alone. It seems nobody can hear her cries...

[*The sound of a collapsing building is heard nearby.*]

BLIND MAN: It was very nearby...

SURVEYOR: [*Still trying to find the spring.*] It is so strange, what has happened to it?

ARCHITECT: It might be our turn at any moment!

SURVEYOR: [*Goes to the* BLIND MAN *cheerfully and picks up the spring from the floor, near his feet.*] I found it! I found it at last!

BLIND MAN: Shush... Be quiet... [*Stands up.*] That Person is approaching...

[*After a few seconds, an old* GNOME *limps into the stage.*]

GNOME: Our number is up...

[*The* BLIND MAN *and* SURVEYOR *go unwillingly toward the* GNOME. *The* ARCHITECT *is still standing.*]

GNOME: [*Approaches the* ARCHITECT.] It is too late now. Come with me.

ARCHITECT: Go away... [*Crouches and sits on the floor.*] No...

Not any more...

GNOME: Poor guy... You have no other choices... You have to die...

[*The sound of several collapsing buildings is heard nearby.*]

GNOME: [*Imperiously.*] Let's go...

BLIND MAN: To establish a new city.

[*Following the* GNOME, *the* BLIND MAN *and* SURVEYOR *exit. The horrible sound of several collapsing buildings echoes through the stage as the whole stage sinks into a deep darkness.*]

WOMAN: [*Calling from different directions, off-stage.*] Is there any one to help me?

FINAL CURTAIN